It was my mother, Barbara, who first saw the Dragon's Blood Tree. 'Quick, quick, come and look at this creature!' she called.

We were wandering around the Botanical Gardens, sticking our noses into flowers. My father and I hurried over – and there it was. Branches twisting together, in and out, over and around, like a demon's knitting, or a magic maze. The Dragon's Blood Tree. Our mouths fell open. We shivered in the sunlight.

'That tree looks like something from a Tashi story,' Barbara said cunningly, and we grinned at each other in delight.

'Here we go again,' said Dad, and rushed off to find us a nice dry spot on the grass where we could all sit down – and begin.

So, if you happen to be wandering around the Botanical Gardens in Sydney, see if you can spot our tree. It is a-maze-ing!

ANNA FIENBERG

Anna and Barbara Fienberg write the Tashi stories together, making up all kinds of daredevil adventures and tricky characters for him to face. Lucky he's such a clever Tashi.

Kim Gamble is one of Australia's favourite illustrators for children. Together Kim and Anna have made such wonderful books as *The Magnificent Nose and Other Marvels*, *The Hottest Boy Who Ever Lived*, the *Tashi* series, the *Minton* picture books, *Joseph*, and a full colour picture book about their favourite adventurer, *There once was a boy called Tashi*.

First published in 1999
This edition first published in 2006

Allen & Unwin
83 Alexander St
Crows Nest NSW 2065
Australia
Phone: (61 2) 8425 0100
Fax: (61 2) 9906 2218
Email: info@allenandunwin.com
Web: www.allenandunwin.com

National Library of Australia
Cataloguing-in-Publication entry:

Fienberg, Anna.
   Tashi and the demons.

   New cover ed.
   For primary school children.
   ISBN 978 174114 970 8.

   ISBN 1 74114 970 3.

   1. Children's stories, Australian. 2. Tashi (Fictitious character) – Juvenile
   fiction. I. Fienberg, Barbara. II. Gamble, Kim. III. Title. (Series: Tashi; 6).

A823.3

Cover and series design by Sandra Nobes
Typeset in Sabon by Tou-Can Design
Printed in Australia by McPhersons Printing Group

10 9 8 7 6 5 4 3 2

Tashi

and the
DEMONS

written by
Anna Fienberg
and
Barbara Fienberg

•

illustrated by
Kim Gamble

ALLEN & UNWIN

One fresh sunny morning, Jack and his
Mum were in the garden, watching Dad
plant a new gardenia bush.

'It's too *early* to be up on Sunday
morning,' Mum yawned.

But Dad couldn't wait to get his new
bush in the ground. 'Mmm,' he said,
putting his nose deep into a flower. 'That
perfume is fantastic!' He stood up, leaning
against his shovel, closing his eyes.

Jack saw an army of bull ants swarm over Dad's gumboots. Must be standing on a nest, he thought. Dad began to hop all over the pansy bed. He hit his shin with the shovel.

'Blasted things've got into my socks!'
he cried.

'Come over here,' said Mum. 'Rest a bit,
it's Sunday!'

Dad peeled off a sock while Mum lay
back in a warm patch of sun. She bunched
her dressing gown under her head.

'Ah, that's better,' she said. 'All we need
now is a story.'

'That gardenia should do well,' said Dad, rubbing his foot. 'After all the rain we've had, the soil is nice and moist.'

'Speaking of rain...' said Jack, settling himself between them.

'A Tashi story, I bet!' cried Mum, sitting up. 'What is it—floods, gushing rivers, monster waves?'

Jack chewed a piece of grass. 'Well, once, in Tashi's old village, it didn't rain for months.'

'No good for *his* gardenias, eh?' said Dad.

'No,' replied Jack. 'It was no good for anything. It hadn't rained for so long that little children could hardly remember the sound of it, or the smell of wet earth. There was almost no rice left in the village, and the last of the chickens and pigs had been eaten ages ago. Every day Tashi's mother sent him a bit further to look for wild spinach or turnips or anything to add to the thin evening stew.'

'Erk!' Dad wrinkled his nose. 'Stew pew!'

'Ssh!' said Mum. 'And leave your foot alone. You'll just make it worse.'

'One day,' Jack went on, 'Tashi had been walking for hours when suddenly he came upon a gooseberry bush, covered with fat fruit. He happily filled his basket and was just cramming the last few berries into his mouth when he heard a cry. There, around the other side of the bush, was a girl.'

'Berry bushes have terrible thorns,' said Dad. 'I expect she'd scratched her hands.'

'I don't think so,' said Jack. 'Tashi just said she was very pretty—sort of shiny and special, like the first evening star.'

'Oh,' said Dad. 'Gosh.'

'Go on,' said Mum breathlessly.

'Well,' Jack continued, 'Tashi saw why the girl was sobbing. Her legs and arms were tied up with ropes. "Who did this? Who are you?" he asked.

'"Oh, please help me," the girl wept. "I am Princess Sarashina, and I'm the prisoner of two horrible demons. They frightened away my guards and dragged me from my travelling coach. They tied me up here two days ago and I've had nothing to eat or drink since then."

'Tashi began undoing the cords around her wrists. He noticed she was looking hungrily into his basket. But when he reluctantly offered her some berries, she said, "Oh no, not now, they might come back any minute. Where can we hide?"

'Tashi thought quickly...behind that
Dragon's Blood Tree? No, it was no use
hiding, he decided. He and the princess
would have to come out some time, and
then what?

'"You go back to my village," he said
finally, "and I'll come later, when I find
some vegetables. I'm very poor and no use
to demons. They won't hurt me."

'"You never know with demons."
Princess Sarashina shook her head. "My
Uncle Lee says demons are like muddy
water. You can never see to the heart of
them and they vanish through your fingers
leaving dirt on your hands. Besides, I don't
know the way to your village."

'"It's easy," said Tashi. "Just follow the
path between those tall trees, go past the
cemetery on your right and then the temple
on your left, over the bridge and there's the
village. Ask for Tashi's house and tell my
parents that I'll be along in a little while.
As for the demons—"

'"Have you ever met one?"

'"I've seen a few in my time," said Tashi. "But never up close."

'"I hope you never do." The Princess shivered. "Their eyes are red as blood, like two whirlpools trying to suck you in. Good luck, Tashi!" And she ran off towards the trees.

'Tashi wandered through the forest, looking out for wild herbs and demons. He found some sorrel and roots and when his hands were full he decided to make his way home. He passed the gooseberry bush and was just checking to see that he hadn't left any berries—he hadn't—when suddenly he was seized by two strong arms and thrown like a ball into the air.

'He looked down into a hideous face.
The eyes were red, just as Sarashina had
said, and inside their scarlet lids the
eyeballs were swirling like flaming mud.
Tashi felt himself being drawn into them,
like a stone into quicksand. With a huge
effort he looked away, staring instead at
teeth hooking over great fleshy lips.

'"Where is Princess Sarashina? What have you done with her?" the demon bellowed. Oh, how Tashi wished he hadn't come back to the gooseberry bush!

'"I haven't done anything to her," he said firmly, just as a second demon came bounding out of the forest. But both demons were now looking hard at Tashi's jacket. There, tucked into a buttonhole, were the cords that he had untied from Sarashina's hands and feet.

'"What are these then? Where is she?" roared the first demon.

'"I won't tell."

'The second demon knocked Tashi to the ground and sat on his chest. He stared deep into Tashi's eyes, but Tashi wouldn't look back. The demon shifted angrily. Then he smiled so all his dagger teeth glinted.

'"I think you *will* tell," he said slowly.

'Tashi didn't like that smile. He thought about demons and Uncle Lee's muddy water, and how you couldn't tell what was at the bottom of it. He knew the demon had a terrible plan, but no matter how hard he tried, Tashi couldn't imagine what it might be. He started to sweat under the demon's heavy legs.

'"I think this will persuade you," the demon said, and he clicked his fingers. A box popped into his hand. "If you don't talk, I am going to tip these spiders over you." He lifted the lid a little to show Tashi what was inside.

'Tashi caught a glimpse of hairy scampering legs and quickly shut his eyes. "I will never tell."

'He pressed his lips together as he felt spiders crawling over his face and up his nose. Taking a deep breath, he tried to still his mind. Yes, that helped. Then, with a great effort, he squeezed out a giggle. "They tickle!"

'The first demon roared with rage. "Give him to me!" He pushed the other demon aside and tied Tashi to a tree with his hands above his head. "Now we'll see how you like *snakes*!"

'He muttered a demon word and a barrel of snakes appeared under the tree. Tashi quivered as snakes slithered over his legs and under his jacket. But he managed to close his eyes, relaxing his muscles and making his mind still.

'"Oh good, snakes!" he cried, grinning. "I have three snakes at home, but they're much bigger than these. I let them sleep at the foot of my bed. Snakes like the warmth, you know."

'The second demon roared with rage. "Give him back to me!" He poked the first demon's chest with a steely finger. "We will never find Princess Sarashina like this—or get the ransom you said the Emperor would pay!"

'Both demons glared at Tashi. Their eyes glowed crimson. Then they turned to each other and hissed one word: "*RATS!*"

'*Wah*, thought Tashi, I *can't* pretend with rats—sharp little yellow teeth, dripping with disease—*ugh!* He took a deep breath. "Rats don't worry me," he said loudly. "In fact, the more there are the better I like it. You can do tricks with rats, you know. Train them with a bit of cheese or meat…I do it all the time at home, with my pets Rattus and Ratz." Tashi smiled broadly at the demons. He was only able to smile, you see, because he'd just thought of a cunning demon trick.'

'That's my boy,' said Dad, looking
relieved. 'I *hate* rats. We had one once in
the kitchen, didn't we, Mum? It gave me
nightmares and chewed my socks.'

'Well,' Jack went on, 'the demons
stamped their feet and jumped about
with fury.

'"Spiders and snakes and rats are really scary!" wailed the first demon. "Humans are supposed to be terrified by them." He grabbed Tashi by the jacket. "Why aren't you? What's wrong with you? What frightens *you*?"

'Tashi bit his lip and made his hands tremble. "The only thing that really scares me," he said, "is getting stuck in a Dragon's Blood Tree. Thank heavens there aren't any in these parts."

'"Ho, ho, that's where you're wrong!" whooped the demons, and they untied him in a flash and dragged him to a tree with branches so thick and twisted together that it was like a magic maze with no beginning nor end.

'"One, two, three, up!" they boomed and the demons tossed Tashi up into the tree.

'"Goodbye, Tashi!" they gloated. "You're trapped now. No one has ever found their way out of a Dragon's Blood Tree, hee hee!"

'But Tashi disappeared.

'The demons waited. "Where did he
go?" asked the first demon uneasily. They
gazed up into the net of branches. Not even
a rat could wiggle out through those. They
bounded back to the gooseberry bush for
a better view of the treetop. Nothing.

'"He's gone!" the demons screamed,
and they jumped into the tree to find him.
They peered and poked about, crawling
over each others' faces as they searched
for Tashi.

'Meanwhile, Tashi wriggled deeper and

deeper into the darkness of the tree. When he came to the centre of the tangled branches, he wound his way down to a hollow in the trunk. With a shiver he slipped inside. It was so black in that tunnel, and tiny soft things flitted past his cheek. The air grew musty and thick. But Tashi kept climbing down, his fingers finding rough holds. His eyes were stinging as he stared into the dark, until at last he spied a faint ray of light. Squeezing through the opening, he crawled on his belly over the roots and ran off home.

'The demons never did find their way out of the Dragon's Blood Tree, and as far as Tashi knows, they are still writhing about in the dark, roaring at each other.'

'And so what happened to the Princess, the one like the evening star?' asked Dad.

'I was just getting to that,' Jack replied. 'Princess Sarashina and Tashi's parents were almost finished their stew of dandelion roots when Tashi burst in the door. His family bombarded him with questions and the Princess was particularly interested in his demon-tricking method.

'"How did you find a way out of the Dragon's Blood Tree?" she asked him admiringly.

'"Wise-as-an-Owl told me," said Tashi. "He's taught me a million things about herbs and plants. Look for the dragon's tunnel at the centre of the trunk, he said, and follow it down till you see the light."

'Princess Sarashina was excited to hear this, and asked if Tashi could introduce her to Wise-as-an-Owl some time. Tashi agreed, and then he walked her down to the river where they found a boat to take her home.

'The next day the boat returned, laden deep in the water with bags of rice and fruit and chickens, enough food to feed the village for the summer. And with the food there was a note saying "Thank you, Tashi" from the Emperor, and an invitation from the Princess for him to visit the palace.

'That night, the villagers decorated Tashi with coloured streamers and carried him around the village on their shoulders. The feasting and laughter grew even louder as clouds blotted out the moon and the rains began to fall.'

Mum and Dad lay on the grass with their eyes closed. They didn't move. Jack looked at their faces. He prodded them.

'We're practising,' said Mum.

'We're trying to still our minds,' said Dad.

'Look, there's a bull ant!' cried Jack, and Dad leapt up as if a bee had stung him.

'Well, better be getting back to my gardenia,' said Dad. 'So when's Tashi coming over, Jack? Maybe he could give me some advice about my plants. What do you think?'

'Sure,' said Jack. 'I'll go and ring him up.'

'And I'll make him some sticky rice cakes,' said Mum. 'In just a minute,' she added, closing her eyes.

THE MAGIC BELL

'Look out, Tashi! Hide behind this tree,
quick!' Jack pulled Tashi down beside him.

'What is it?'

'Look, *there*.' Jack pointed to the veranda of number 42. An old man leant over the balcony. He had wild curly hair and a cockatoo on his shoulder. He didn't look very dangerous to Tashi. But then Tashi had seen a lot of evil and calamitous things in his time, it was true.

'That's Mr B. J. Curdle. He's always pestering me,' hissed Jack. 'I'm just walking home from school, right—like now, minding my own business—and out dashes old Curdle, stopping me and asking *how I am*.'

Tashi frowned. 'What's so terrible about that?'

'Well, he makes these dreadful homemade medicines from plants in his garden, and he wants to try them out on *me*! Once, I felt sorry for him—his cockatoo had a limp—so I went in. Instead of lemonade he gave me this thick yellow stuff to drink. He said it was strengthening medicine. Yuk!'

'And did it make you strong?'

'You've got to be kidding! That mixture made me weak as a baby—it tasted like mashed cockroaches. I felt like throwing up all the way home. The man's a menace!'

When the old man had gone back inside, and the two boys were walking home, Tashi said, 'What you need is a Magic Warning Bell, like the one we had in my village. It rang whenever danger was near.'

'Ooh, that *would* be handy. What did it look like?'

'Well, it was very old and beautiful, the most precious thing we had in the village. When dragons came over the mountain it would ring out, and once, when a giant wandered near, its clanging was so deafening that even people working in the fields had time to escape. Lucky for me, it rang the day the River Pirate arrived.'

Jack stopped on the path. 'Oh, I remember *him*—he was that really fierce pirate you tricked with a bag of fake gold.'

Tashi nodded. 'I had to, or I'd have been carved up like a turkey. But I always knew when he discovered it he would come back to get me.'

Jack shivered. 'So what did he do?'

'Well, it was like this,' said Tashi. 'I was in the village square getting some water from the well when the bell tolled softly. It seemed to be ringing just for me.

'I stood there, frozen, trying to think.
But all I could see in my mind was that
Pirate, stroking the end of his sword.
I sipped some water. That helped. I decided
that the first place he'd look for me would
be my house, so I dropped my bucket and
ran to my cousin Wu, who lived high up on
a hill overlooking the village.

'From Wu's front window I could see the River Pirate tying up his boat. Just the sight of him gave me the shivers. He was *huge*— the muscles in his arms were like boulders. I watched him stride along the jetty, turning into the road ... he was heading straight for my house! My mother told him she didn't know where I was, but he banged about inside anyway, frightening her and my grandparents. He knocked a pot of soup off the fire and kicked over a table, then went charging about the village asking for me.'

Jack kicked a stone ferociously. 'They'd better not tell him where you were!'

'Well, a few villagers had seen me running up to Wu's house, but they all said they had no idea where I'd gone. Still, there was one little boy who didn't understand the danger I was in. He skipped up to the River Pirate calling, "Do you want to know where Tashi is? Well—" but at that moment three large women sat on him.

'"Well *what*?" growled the River Pirate.

'"Well so do we," the women replied, and the Pirate scowled and hurried on. He searched all day, growing more and more angry. People ran into their houses and locked the doors, but he threw rocks at their windows and tore up their gardens. That night, on his way back to the boat, the River Pirate stole the Magic Bell.'

'Oh no!' cried Jack.

'Oh yes!' said Tashi. 'The next morning,
when they noticed that the bell was gone,
the people were very upset. The Baron told
everyone that it was my fault because I had
tricked the River Pirate in the first place.
People began to give me hard looks. They
said that the bell had hung over the well
since Time began and now, because of me,
the village had lost its special warning.
Some little children threw stones at me and
their parents looked the other way. I felt so
miserable I could have just sat down in a
field and never got up.

'So I went to see Wise-as-an-Owl, to ask his advice. He was busy at his workbench when I walked in, filling jars with herbs and plants.

' "Ah, Tashi," he smiled as I came in. He looked at me for a moment. "You'd better help yourself to some willowbark juice over there." '

Jack shuddered. 'What's that? Does it taste like mashed cockroaches?'

'No,' said Tashi. 'But it can cure head-aches. I've learnt everything I know about plants and potions from Wise-as-an-Owl—he's an expert on the medicine plants of the mountain and forest. So I told him yes, I would have a dose, because I *did* have a pounding headache and a terrible problem.

'Of course Wise-as-an-Owl knew all about the River Pirate. He'd watched him stamping all over his herb garden out the front. "Go and face the villain, Tashi," he told me. "It will go better if *you* find *him* first."

'He gave me two packets of special herbs to keep in my pocket. "Wolf's breath and jindaberry," he said. "Remember what I've taught you and mind how you use them."

'I thanked him and looked around for the last time at the plants and jars and pots of dandelion and juniper boiling on the stove. Then I set out for the city at the mouth of the river. There I would find the River Pirate.

'I walked for two days, and as I trudged through forests and waded through streams, I thought about what I should say to him. On the last night, lying under the stars, I decided that I'd try to make a bargain with him. What I'd offer him would be fair, and would mean a big sacrifice for me!

'I had no trouble finding the River Pirate down in the harbour. He was sitting at the end of the jetty with his black-hearted crew.

You could hear them from miles away. They were dangling their legs over the side, passing a bucket of beer to each other and shouting and singing rude pirate songs at the tops of their voices. Every now and then they would tear great hunks of meat from a freshly roasted pig—stolen, you could be sure.'

'"There you are, you treacherous young devil!" the River Pirate spluttered when he saw me, leaping up and showering my face with greasy gobbets of pig. He grabbed my arm and yanked me toward him. His hand flew to his sword.

'"Wait!" I cried. "Listen!" I took a deep breath to stop my voice from trembling. Suddenly I had terrible doubts that a River Pirate could care about people being fair or making sacrifices, but it was the only idea I'd had. "If I work for you for a year and a day," I said boldly, "will you give back the bell?"

'The River Pirate just laughed. He threw back his great bony head and roared, "I will keep you for *ten* years and a day—and the bell as well!" Then the crew grabbed me and tossed me into the boat.

'By sunset we'd set sail. When the first star glittered in the sky, the cook told me to go down into the galley and start chopping mountains of fish and vegetables. And every day after that I had to do the same arm-aching jobs. The cook was spiteful and the work was hard and boring—except when it was frightening. Like the time another pirate ship attacked us.'

'*Enemy* pirates?' cried Jack. 'What did you use as a weapon—your kitchen knife?'

'Well,' said Tashi, 'it was like this. One moonless night, a swarm of bawling, yelling-for-blood pirates sprang onto our boat. They took us completely by surprise. Where could I hide? I glanced frantically around the boat and spied a big coil of rope. I scuttled over and buried myself in the rope just as the enemy Captain bounded up. He was barking orders and threats like a mad dog when he suddenly caught sight of the River Pirate. Swiping at the air with his sword, he gave a vicious battle cry—and tripped over me! *Wah!* I shivered when I looked up into his face, but he didn't hesitate for a moment. He picked me up as if I were just a weevilly old crust and flicked me overboard.

'Lucky for me there was a rope ladder hanging from the side of the boat. I grabbed it and swung down, clinging onto the last rung as I dangled in the black and icy water.

'My fingers were stiffening with cold and it was hard to hang onto the fraying strands of rope. Something slithery kept twining around my legs! I kicked hard and looked down into the dark waves. A giant octopus was staring up at me, its tentacles groping for my ankle. Then, to my horror, I felt my shoe being sucked from my foot!

'At that very moment, just when it seemed that my mother would never see her precious boy again, I heard the River Pirate and his men bellowing out their song of victory. I could hear the dreadful splash as enemy pirates were thrown over the side.

'Oh, how wet and wretched I was when I climbed back into the boat. But all I got was the River Pirate's ranting fury. "Why didn't that mangy magic bell ring to warn us?" he shouted, as he wiped the blood of an enemy pirate from his eye.

'"It only rings for the place where it belongs," I told him, and he scowled so deeply that his eyebrows met in the middle.

'The next morning, I saw three pirates racing up to the deck to be sick over the side. By afternoon two more men and the cook looked quite green. They wobbled around as if their legs were made of noodles. As our village came into sight, I said to the River Pirate, "If I can cure your men of their sickness, will you let me go?"

'"No!" snarled the Pirate, but just then he bent over and clutched his stomach.

"Aaargh, I'm dying ... Go on then, but be quick," he gasped.

'I slipped down to the galley where I had hidden my packets of medicine plants. Quickly I threw some into a pot and boiled them up.

'The men only needed a few mouthfuls each before they stopped rolling about on the deck and sat up. One even smiled. The River Pirate was hanging over the side of the boat like a piece of limp seaweed, but he turned his head and begged for me to hurry.

'"And will you give me back the bell as well?" I asked him. The River Pirate ground his teeth. I tilted the pot a little. "I hope I don't spill these last few spoonfuls," I worried.

'"Ah, take the bell, take it. It doesn't work anyway," the River Pirate hissed.

'And so that's how I came back to the village with the magic bell.'

Tashi looked at Jack and laughed. 'Do you realise we've walked right past your house and mine?'

'Well,' said Jack, grinning, 'come back to my place and have a glass of lemonade. Or we could always call in on Mr Curdle if you'd prefer...But tell me, what happened when you got home?'

'The villagers all crowded around, welcoming me and saying they were sorry for their harsh words. But when I took the bell out of the sack, there was a great shout and people threw their hats in the air. We hung the bell back on its hook over the well. And then—something that had never happened before—it gave a joyful peal!'

'Gee,' said Jack, 'wasn't it lucky that the pirates got sick so that they needed your medicine!'

Tashi smiled. 'I think Wise-as-an-Owl would tell you that luck had nothing to do with it. Sometimes medicines that make you sick are almost as useful as those that make you well.'

'Aha!' said Jack, giving Tashi a knowing look, and they leapt up the steps of Jack's house, two at a time.